Rosalyn Thompson

This Is Your Life

Part 1

Dedicated to all the school girls and their school girl crew

(Episode 1)

The Move

"Mama why do we have to move? I don't want to go to a new school and I don't want to leave my friends."

"Look Rosalyn we've had this conversation more than a million times. Your dad's promotion means more money and it also means we have to move closer to the city. Besides, we'll only be a few minutes away from grandma and you can always make new friends."

Rosalyn didn't say another word. Now was not a good time to get on her mother's nerves. The last moving van had already left and she and her mother would be making the hour and half drive to Sherwood as soon as they finished locking up the old house. Rosalyn's dad had gone to the new house a few days earlier to get settled in and make sure things were comfortable for her and her mother when they arrived.

She had been dreading this day ever since her dad came home six months ago with the news about his promotion and "the big move". There were so many "didn'ts" that surrounded the whole situation for Rosalyn. She didn't want to move to a new neighborhood. She didn't want to go to a new school and she certainly didn't want to make new friends. She would miss her old friends especially Monica who had been her best friend since the second grade. But it was too late now. The day had come to move and Rosalyn felt like her world was being yanked from beneath her.

It wasn't fair she thought. She had lived in Caymen Point her whole life and now, the summer before her eighth-grade year, her dad gets this big promotion that's supposed to be "*good for everyone in the family*".

Her parents' arguments for moving right outside the city were there would be a lot more events which was good for her mom's catering business. The move would also give Rosalyn a chance to be exposed to the culture and diversity that a big city offers and her dad would finally be a Senior Advisor at the corporate office of his architect firm and making a lot more money. The best thing about the move is that they all would be able to see grandma more. None of these arguments comforted Rosalyn and neither did her dad's suggestion of visiting Monica whenever she wanted.

As her mom backed the car out of the driveway, Rosalyn gazed out of the window of the passenger seat. Her eyes began to swell and make way for the warm tears that streamed down her toffee colored cheeks.

"Listen sweetie," said Rosalyn's mom in a soft voice. "I know this move is hard for you and it might be tough at first, but I assure you, It'll get easier. Besides, this move is good for all of us."

Yeah right, thought Rosalyn as they made their way through the streets of her old neighborhood and on to the freeway.

It had only been three days since the move and Rosalyn had already talked to Monica 12 times. She was even more convinced that she would never get used to this whole thing. Despite the warm summer days, which would have normally sent her dashing to the pool with her friends back in Caymen Point, Rosalyn stayed in the house mostly in her room watching movies or listening to music. It made it a little easier that her new room was bigger than her old one. Also, she did have to admit that the new house was nicer than the old one too. She knew one day

7

she would have to go out into the real world but she just wasn't ready yet.

"Roz I need you to walk to the corner store for me," her mom yelled from the kitchen downstairs. "I really need to finish frying this fish before your grandma gets here and I'm pretty sure I won't have enough cornmeal. You know how she loves fried catfish and potato salad and I want everything to be ready when she gets here."

"Oh mama do I have to?" Rosalyn yelled backed.

"Yes you have to. You wouldn't want to disappoint your grandma would you? Besides, It'll do you some good to get out of this house and get some fresh air. You've been mopin' around long enough."

"But ma I..."

"Don't but ma me young lady! You know better than that!"

Her mother's words and tone of voice let her know that the issue wasn't up for discussion. She'd better start making her way downstairs quick. This was one of the disadvantages of being an only child.

Whenever her parents wanted something done there was only one person to do it... Rosalyn.

Since she had no intentions on leaving the house or seeing anyone other than her grandma, she hadn't bothered getting dressed earlier. Rosalyn quickly dug through one of the boxes that were still packed and pulled out a wrinkled navy blue tank top.

"This will do," she mumbled to herself as she held up the shirt and briefly examined it for stains. Rosalyn wasn't up for going out into the neighborhood let alone possibly even meeting someone, so she really didn't care what she looked like. She slipped on a pair of old khaki shorts and white canvas sneakers and pulled her single braids up into a sloppy ponytail with a black hair tie. When she came downstairs and into the kitchen her mother looked at her awkwardly.

"Girl I hope you don't run into your prince charming down at the corner store cause if you do he'll probably turn and gallop off the other way," her mother remarked laughing.

"Mama you know I don't want to do this so please don't make it any harder than it already is," whined Rosalyn.

"I know lovebug. I was just joking and trying to lighten you up," her mom said still smiling.

Rosalyn's mom had a quick wit, a great sense of humor and was well educated among other things. She had a kind yet strong personality (you wouldn't want to get on her bad side) and she loved to cook. She took pride in the fact that she owned her own catering business. Rosalyn knew she could talk to her mom about almost anything. Her mother was a good listener who understood Rosalyn's problems most of the time and she was always right.

It was a lot warmer outside than she had thought but then again how could she tell after being locked up inside the house for three days. As Rosalyn aimlessly walked along the streets of her new neighborhood, she realized it was actually a nice place. Of course she wouldn't let her parents know she felt this way. There were lots of big trees that lined the streets and every house had its own special characteristics, unlike her old neighborhood where every house looked the same. Here in Sherwood some houses were pink, some were blue and some were that plain ugly brown that every neighborhood has.

As she made her way closer to the store she could see two girls huddled in a corner laughing. They didn't see her at first because they seemed to be looking down at a picture that one of them was holding. As Rosalyn approached the front door of the store they both looked up. Rosalyn put her head down remembering her hair, wrinkled tank top and faded shorts. She wasn't in the mood to make new friends and she certainly wasn't dressed for the occasion. Her first thought was to turn and go back home and tell her mom the store was out of cornmeal but then she remembered something her mother had often told her.

> *"If you want people to respect you, you have to be brave enough to look them in the eyes and demand their respect."*

Yes, that's the only thing she wanted. Their respect. She didn't want their friendship because she had her own friends back in Caymen Point. The only thing she did want was to let them know that just because she was the new kid in the neighborhood she wasn't afraid of them. She slowly lifted her head and looked them both in their eyes. One of them was the color of dark brown sugar and the other was a lighter caramel color. The darker one had what some black people called "good hair", kind of wavy and smooth. The other was wearing a trendy fishing cap so Rosalyn couldn't tell what kind of hair she had. One of them smiled and the other stared blankly. Rosalyn managed a slight smile and made her way into the store. She hoped they would be gone when she came out.

(Episode 2)

The Meeting

    The corner store smelled of air conditioning coolant and old pastries. Rosalyn wandered from aisle to aisle looking for the cornmeal. She finally found it on the aisle with the cooking oil and flour. As she made her way to the cashier and glanced out the double glass doors marked "EXIT", she could see the two girls were still standing outside the store. *Were they waiting for her? What did they want? Did they want to be her friend or her enemy?* Whatever their reasons, Rosalyn had decided she would walk out the store and look straight ahead. She had already done more than she had wanted to when she smiled at them.

She paid the cashier and walked out of the store looking straight ahead. Soon after, she heard a voice call out behind her.

"Hey are you new around here?"

Rosalyn kept walking and pretended not to hear.

"Maybe she didn't hear you Sharice. Ask her again," said the one without the hat.

"Hey you with the braids in your hair."

Rosalyn turned and looked as if it was a bother.

"Are you new to the neighborhood?", the girl said again.

"Yeah, I guess you could say that," Rosalyn replied as unfriendly as she could and turned and walked away.

The walk back home seemed a lot shorter than the one on the way to the store. Rosalyn walked in the house and dropped the box of cornmeal on the kitchen counter. Her mother was standing at the sink cutting potatoes for the potato salad. As Rosalyn left the kitchen to go back up to her room she bumped into her dad.

"Oh hi daddy! You scared me. I didn't know you were home."

"I'm sorry pumpkin. I didn't mean to scare you but I heard the front door and I was hoping it was you. Your mother told me you finally came out of that dungeon and went out into the land of the living. It wasn't too bad now was it?"

"Well it certainly isn't Caymen Point that's for sure," grumbled Rosalyn.

"What exactly do you mean by that," asked her dad.

"Never mind daddy. You wouldn't understand."

Just then the doorbell rang.

"Oh, that must be your grandmother," her father said as he went to open the door.

To Rosalyn's surprise a few moments later her dad called out, "Rosalyn there's someone at the door for you."

For me! thought Rosalyn. *Who in the world could this be!*

"Rosalyn, did you hear me?" her dad called out again. "There's someone here for you. She says her name is Sharice and that she met you down at the corner store."

OH---MY---GOD! she thought. *How did she know where I lived?*

"Okay I'm coming daddy," She yelled back nervously.

When Rosalyn got to the door the girl with the fishing hat was standing there with a polite smile on her face.

"I'm sorry I followed you," said the girl. "But you forgot to tell me your name."

"No, I didn't forget," Rosalyn replied rudely. "I just didn't tell you…but anyway it's Rosalyn. Rosalyn Thompson."

"Okay well hi again. My name is Sharice. Sharice Phillips."

"I know," said Rosalyn bluntly. "I heard your friend say your name down at the store."

"Oh, you mean Zoey," said the girl.

"Yeah I guess that's her." Rosalyn was making it very clear that she didn't care about making a new friend.

After a few awkward moments had passed the girl spoke again.

"Well I just stopped to get your name since I didn't get it earlier. You think you might wanna hang out sometime?"

"I don't know. Maybe," said Rosalyn.

"Okay, well I guess I'll see you around."

"Yeah, see ya," said Rosalyn as she shut the front door.

"My goodness, you didn't make that easy for her did you?" said her dad.

"That's because I have my own friends back in Caymen Point daddy," said Rosalyn.

"Roz, that's just it," her dad said sincerely. "Your old friends are back in Caymen Point and you're not. Eventually you're going to have to make new friends here in Sherwood."

Rosalyn didn't say another word and went up to her room to wait for her grandma.

(Episode 3)

The Visit

The visit with grandma was well worth it. She came with gifts for everyone in the family. Mrs. Thompson received new cutlery for cooking, Rosalyn's gift was a pink teddy bear with money stuffed in the ribbon around its neck and Mr. Thompson received a brand new black leather wallet. Rosalyn's grandma was always making fun of how old and rugged her son's wallet was and how it was a miracle that he could carry anything in it without losing it.

"You know Dennis, it's a wonder you have any money at all with the way that thing looks. No one should ever have to pick your pockets," she would say laughing. "All they have to do is walk

behind you and wait for yo belongings to come fallin'
out."

Rosalyn's grandmother was fun and pretty hip
for an old lady. She could always make Rosalyn laugh
with her jokes and stories from the "good 'ol days".
Since Rosalyn was her only grandchild in the state of
California, she pretty much had her grandmother all
to herself, especially now that they lived only a few
minutes away. Rosalyn figured this would be the only
friend outside of Caymen Point she would ever have.

After her grandma finished two helpings of
what she called "some screamin' catfish" and potato
salad, the four of them went into the family room for
their usual family conversation.

"So, how's my most favorite granddaughter in
all the state of Cali been doin'?" said Rosalyn's
grandmother as she sat down on the sofa.

"Grandma I'm your only granddaughter in all
the state of Cali," Rosalyn replied.

"Well even if you weren't, I'm almost sure
you'd still be my favorite," said her grandma with a
huge smile. "Have you met any new friends yet?"

Rosalyn's mom and dad looked at each other and then at Rosalyn and waited for her answer.

"Well, no not really. Besides, I don't need any new friends grandma. My old ones are just fine," she said trying to sound cheerful.

"I know you have your old friends baby," said her grandma sounding concerned. "But you need to make some new ones here in Sherwood. With that charming personality and beautiful smile I know you'll have a whole gang of friends in no time. In the meantime, why don't you come and go to church with me tomorrow. How's that sound?"

"Sounds good I guess," Rosalyn said unsure of herself.

"Of course it sounds good! It sounds great!", her dad said enthusiastically. "You've been locked up in this house for four days and…"

"It's only been three days daddy. Today doesn't count because I had to go to the store for cornmeal."

"Excuse me. Three days," her dad said sarcastically.

"Well then it's settled. It's me and my grandbaby tomorrow in the Lord's house," her grandma said and chuckled.

(Episode 4)

The Surprise

The next morning Rosalyn put on a long, brown stretch knit skirt with a short-sleeved white cardigan sweater set. She figured she didn't have to get too dressed up since she was only going to be around a bunch of church-going old people. Her grandma picked her up at ten thirty sharp for the eleven o' clock Sunday service. They stopped at the corner store to get plenty of church candy to snack on throughout the service.

When they walked into the church lobby Rosalyn could hear the sound of people singing church hymns and hands clapping. A few moments later she was suddenly hit with the smell of stale perfume and menthol candy. A lady in a white, fancy, feathered hat cheerfully greeted her grandma.

"How you doin' this Sunday mornin' Sista Thompson?"

"Oh I'm just fine," replied Rosalyn's grandma equally as cheerful. "Can't complain so long as the Lord keep waking me up every day. What about 'chew?".

"I'm doin' pretty good," said the lady. "Who's that pretty girl you got with you?"

"Oh lord where are my manners! Sista Banks, this here is my granddaughter Rosalyn. Her and her parents just moved here from Caymen Point," said Rosalyn's grandmother proudly.

"Well hello Rosalyn," said the lady politely.

"Hi," replied Rosalyn trying to smile.

"How you like it here in Sherwood so far?"

"It's okay," said Rosalyn.

"You don't sound too enthused about our little city," replied the lady.

"That's only because she hasn't met any friends yet," Rosalyn's grandmother interrupted. "But I'm sure that will change soon, right Rosalyn?"

"Right grandma," replied Rosalyn somewhat embarrassed. She knew her grandmother meant well but she really didn't have to broadcast it to all of Sherwood that she was the new kid around without a friend.

"Well I think there's something we can do about that!" the lady said excited. "I have a niece about your age and as a matter of fact she's probably back in the social hall right now. She watches the little ones during the service. Come and follow me and I'll take you to her!"

Rosalyn's grandma smiled at her and quickly grabbed her by the hand. They followed the lady eagerly around the back of the church to the social hall. Her grandmother didn't even ask her if she wanted to meet this girl but the way Rosalyn saw it she really didn't have a choice.

"Zoey" the lady yelled over the small children's voices. "Come on over here. I have someone I want you to meet."

Rosalyn couldn't believe it. It was the other girl from the store! Her heart stopped beating briefly and she suddenly wished she had taken more time

25

getting dressed this morning. This was the second time she had run into this girl without looking her best.

"Zoey this here is Rosalyn and she's new here in Sherwood,"

"Hi," Rosalyn and the girl said in unison pretending it was their first time seeing each other.

"I figured the two of you could get more acquainted while we go enjoy the service," said the lady. "Zoey be sure and give her a dose of some good 'ol Banks family hospitality."

"I will Aunt Lola," replied Zoey in a girlish high pitched tone.

"Well, I guess I'll see you later," said Rosalyn's grandmother with a huge smile and friendly wink of the eye.

"Okay grandma," Rosalyn's mouth said but her head pleaded *'don't leave me here with this girl'*. As the two women turned and left, Rosalyn and Zoey stood in an awkward silence. After a few moments one of them spoke.

"So where you from?" Zoey's voice changed to a deeper, more mature tone.

"Caymen Point," replied Rosalyn as one of the little girls stood beside her pulling on her skirt.

"Tiffany go somewhere and sit down!" Zoey yelled at the little girl.

"Where in the heck is Caymen Point?"

"It's about an hour east from here."

"What grade you goin' to?"

"Eighth," replied Rosalyn.

"Oh good. That means you're right with me and Sharice. She told me she came to your house and you said you might wanna hang some time. I really wasn't looking forward to spending my last year at Kennedy hangin' out with some 6th or 7th grader. I'm glad we're all in the same grade. So you got a boyfriend?"

"No, I do not have a boyfriend," Rosalyn snapped. Zoey's prying questions were starting to get on her nerves. "Why?"

"Just asking," answered Zoey.

You mean just being nosy, thought Rosalyn.

"Do *you* have a boyfriend?"

"Girl yes, of course!" blurted out Zoey. "Zoey Banks without a man? I don't think so! He's *fine* too. His name is Jarell Taylor. You wanna see a picture of him?

"Sure," replied Rosalyn half-heartedly. When she looked at the picture of the boy he didn't look so cute to her. He had big ears and an extra-long forehead. This must have been the picture her and Sharice were looking at the other day. No wonder they were laughing thought Rosalyn. This boy was dirt *ugly*.

"Ain't he fine?"

"Uhh huh," lied Rosalyn.

"You won't have any trouble here in Sherwood finding you a cute man. We have plenty of them," gloated Zoey. "You'll see when school starts."

As Rosalyn listened to Zoey talk about finding a boyfriend, she realized that hanging out with this girl could probably get her into a lot of trouble. Rosalyn was not the least bit interested in having a boyfriend. If Jarell Taylor was any indication of what the rest of the boys looked like in Sherwood, then she certainly didn't want one. Besides, her parents would kill her.

For the rest of the day she listened to Zoey talk about who was the "in" crowd and who was the "out" crowd and how she should probably only hang around her and Sharice to be safe. Zoey talked about all the best places to hang out and had somehow convinced Rosalyn that it was in her best interest to come with her and Sharice to the skating rink that evening. She informed Rosalyn it was *the* place to be and as she put it "everybody and their mama would be there". By the time Rosalyn's grandma picked her up, she knew more about life in Sherwood than she'd wanted to.

(Episode 5)

The Fall

Zoey was right. The skating rink was packed with dozens of giggling girls her age and just as many boys. Some skated around the rink to the latest tunes as disco lights circled the semi-dark room. Rosalyn didn't have to ask her parents twice that evening about going. When they heard the news about her spending time with some newfound friends, they were so enthused they practically demanded that she go. Her grandma was even more excited since she would be hanging out with some "good wholesome church girls".

They had gotten there just early enough to get the last table in the snack bar area.

"So you guise want to get something to drink before we hit the rink?" asked Sharice.

"That sounds good," replied Zoey. "Why don't you go get the sodas and I'll go get our skates. Rosalyn you can stay here and save our table."

"Alright," said Rosalyn. Although she agreed to stay at the table, she felt a little uncomfortable being alone. As soon as the two girls walked away Rosalyn felt like everyone was staring at her. She kept her head up and tried to look comfortable but her efforts failed when she saw a group of girls staring at her. She was relieved when she saw Sharice walking back to the table with a tray of sodas.

"Oh, I see you've been noticed by the goonie bunch," said Sharice with a frown on her face. "Girl don't even worry about wasting your time with them. They will use you and abuse you."

"Oh yeah, well I wish they would stop looking at me like I'm an alien or something," Rosalyn said as she picked up her soda and began to drink. Just then

Zoey returned with the skates and a sly smile on her face.

"There are some cuties in the house tonight!" she blurted out.

"Are boys the only thing you ever think about," asked Sharice.

"No, they are not. Don't get all mad at me just because you're and old maid. You've never even kissed a boy before. And don't $EVEN$ try to count the time Jamaal Smith kissed you in the tanbark in the second grade," laughed Zoey.

"I thought you already had a boyfriend Zoey?" said Rosalyn.

"She does but you'll soon find out that doesn't mean a thing to her," said Sharice putting her skates on.

They all skated together circling the rink to the sounds of the latest hip hop tunes. Rosalyn caught herself smiling and having a good time with Sharice and Zoey until she found herself lying on the rink floor with some boy lying on top of her. The boy had run smack dab into Rosalyn while goofing off with his friends and had knocked her over and fell right on top of her.

"Why don't you watch where the heck you're going you jerk!" yelled Sharice as she pushed the boy to the side and helped Rosalyn get up. Rosalyn was speechless. She could hear some of the kids laughing as both her and the boy got up and dusted themselves off. She was so embarrassed she skated straight to her seat.

"Rosalyn are you okay?"

"Oh she's fine Sharice stop having a cow," said Zoey. "She just had a little accident with Mr. Johnson… That is *Kevin Johnson*," she said laughing.

"Look you guise go ahead without me. I'm gonna sit down and rest for a minute," Rosalyn said. She couldn't believe this had happened. She wanted to go home and she wanted to go home now. There was still an hour left and she didn't want to ruin the fun for Sharice and Zoey.

"Rosalyn are you sure you're okay? We'll sit with you if you want us to," said Sharice.

"No *we* won't. I'm goin' back out there to get my skate on!" snapped Zoey. "Besides, I wouldn't mind being knocked down by Kevin myself."

"I'm fine really. You two go ahead," said Rosalyn.

As the two girls went back out to skate, Rosalyn felt a sudden longing to be with her best friend Monica. Monica would know exactly how to cheer her up but those days were over. She had to make the best of her life in Sherwood. She decided to stop feeling sorry for herself and went back skating when her two new friends came back to check on her. When she thought about it, Kevin *was* kinda cute.

(Episode 6)

Just Business

It had only been a week since the skating rink incident and Rosalyn, Sharice and Zoey had already been to the movies twice, to the mall to hang out and swimming at the Sherwood City Park pool. Life in Sherwood was starting to seem almost normal.

"Roz, please come and get this phone girl, it has been ringing off the hook all morning!" yelled Rosalyn's mom. "And you need to hurry and get dressed if you're going with me to the catering show."

"Okay ma, I'm coming!" Rosalyn replied. She ran out of the bathroom to get the phone in the hallway so she could have some privacy. Sharice and Zoey had already called her several times this morning. They heard from Shauna Sims' best friends' cousin Tina, who just happened to be at the skating rink Sunday, that Kevin Johnson might like Rosalyn. They had been doing some investigating on the issue and kept calling Rosalyn with gossip updates.

She picked up the phone and waited until she heard her mom hang up before she said anything.

"Hello."

"Yeah Rosalyn, guess what. It's true girl! It's all over town that Kevin has a thing for you!" Zoey shouted excitedly.

"Look, I told you guise earlier that I'm not the least bit interested in Kevin Johnson or anybody else," replied Rosalyn.

"I don't blame you. You are too smart and too cute to be with the likes of Kevin or any of those other fools in his crew," said Sharice.

"Oh shut up Sharice!" shouted Zoey. "You just want everybody to be alone like you."

"Everyone doesn't have to be tied down to some little snot nosed boy in order to feel like a complete person Zoey. I'm totally happy with just being a friend to the both of you without having to deal with some boy," argued Sharice.

"Save that good Samaritan speech for someone else. All I know is Kevin Johnson likes Rosalyn and she better jump on him if she wants him because he won't last long," said Zoey.

After listening to the two girls go back and forth with each other Rosalyn jumped in.

"Listen guise, I wish I could sit and chat but I have to go and get dressed. I'm going to some big catering show with my mom downtown. I'll call you when I get home."

"What do you mean you'll call us when you get home," snapped Zoey. "We need to know what to tell him!"

"Look Zoey, I told you how I feel. Tell him whatever you want, I don't care. All I know is I have to go. My mom is calling me. Bye," said Rosalyn and hung up the phone.

This was Rosalyn's first time going with her mom to a show and her first time being in downtown

Sherwood. She was intrigued with the way this part of town was very much like a big city. There were a few skyscrapers and lots of small shops, boutiques, hotels and restaurants. Back in Caymen Point, the closest thing they had to a city atmosphere was a strip mall with a few restaurants and shops.

The catering show was in the banquet room of some fancy hotel with lots of flower arrangements and tall statues. There were a lot of people and hundreds of deli trays, huge casseroles, fruit dishes and meat displays. The smell was enough to make your mouth water.

Rosalyn thought it was interesting the way her mother mingled around the room with other people in her line of work. As she followed her mom around and listened to her talk with restaurant owners and food companies about *distribution* and *food to person ratio*, her mom seemed even more in control and smarter than before. It was obvious that she already knew a lot of the people because some of them addressed her as "Terry" instead of "Teresa Thompson".

"Well hello Terry. It's been a while since I've seen you at a show."

"Hello Dana. Yes it has been a while but that's only because I've been so busy with work and all. I don't have as much time as I used to," Rosalyn's mom replied with a smile. For some reason, she didn't bother introducing Rosalyn to Dana like she had so eagerly done with everyone else.

"Is that right," snapped the woman. "Well I haven't heard your name being mentioned around town with any of the *major events*."

Rosalyn was beginning to realize that this lady and her mom weren't very good friends. She certainly had never heard her mom mention her name before. And who did she think she was talking to her mom this way. After that last remark she glanced over at her mother and waited for her reply. She knew her mom wasn't going to stand for this.

"Well you know Dana, when you get really good at what you do you don't have to go *begging* for work. Good work comes to you. I've been doing a lot of the more private and expensive affairs that aren't open to the public. That's probably why you

39

haven't heard about them," her mom said still smiling and obviously insulting Dana.

"Is that so?"

"Yeah that's so. Well it's been nice seeing you again. Maybe I'll see you around some time or maybe not. Ready Roz?"

"Ready," Rosalyn said.

"Yeah me too," said her mom and they both walked away smiling while Dana stood there with her mouth hanging open.

"Mama who was that lady?" asked Rosalyn when they reached the hotel lobby.

"No one important. Just a bad blast from the past. I'll tell you about it over lunch," said her mom as they made their way to the car.

They decided to have lunch at the cheese steak place two blocks from where the hotel was. They sat and ate their order of garlic fries and supreme style cheese steak sandwiches while Rosalyn's mom filled her in on little Miss Dana from the catering show.

It turns out that Dana and her mom had actually been good friends at one time when they both were just starting out in the catering business. They worked together for about two years and were just about to go in as partners when Dana up and left one day. She went and started her own business taking all the recipes with her including the one's Mrs. Thompson had created herself. Of course that didn't stop her mom from going ahead with her dream of becoming one of the best known caterers in the business. Mrs. Thompson came up with a new and improved marketing plan along with new recipes. Soon she became extremely popular and gained a long list of clients. This made it difficult for anyone who had anything similar to her style, such as Dana, to make a name for themselves. Rosalyn's mom said that "Miss Thing" has been bitter ever since.

"You know Roz, people like Dana will never be happy. She's willing to do whatever she thinks it takes get to the top, even if it means selling her soul to the devil himself," said Mrs. Thompson.

"Mama what do you mean by selling her soul to the devil?"

"What I mean is she'll sacrifice her beliefs for what she wants and doesn't care who she hurts.

Rosalyn don't ever let go of what you believe in and what you've been taught is right," said her mom looking directly at her. "Your beliefs are what make you who you are. Once you lose them you lose yourself."

"So you think Dana has lost herself?"

"A long time ago sweetie," said Rosalyn's mom picking up her purse. "But enough about her. All this talk about Dana is ruining my day with you. Let's blow this joint!"

"Blow this joint?" Rosalyn said laughing.

"Yeah, you know. Get out of here. Go home."

"Mama, really. I have got to bring you up to date on the latest slang," said Rosalyn. They both laughed and made their way to the door.

Just as they were about to push the door open and walk out, a tall man and a boy who must have been his son, opened the door to walk in. The man held the door open for them as they walked out.

"Thank you," said Mrs. Thompson who walked out first.

As Rosalyn made her way out behind her mom, she quickly glanced to see if the boy was anyone she recognized from hanging out with Zoey and Sharice. When she looked up she couldn't believe her eyes. It was Kevin! They briefly glanced at each other from the corner of their eyes and quickly looked down to avoid eye contact. Rosalyn had meant to say thank you but her mouth wouldn't move. She quickened her step to catch up with her mom. As she got inside the car she had butterflies in her stomach and her heart was beating so loud she thought her mother might hear it. Rosalyn must have looked dazed because her mom took notice.

"Roz are you okay? You don't look so good."

"Uh, yeah I'm fine," replied Rosalyn. *Why am I reacting this way* she thought. *I don't even like Kevin.*

"Are you sure you're okay? It might have been the food you ate," said her mom.

"No mama I'm fine, really."

Mrs. Thompson drove home enjoying the sounds of Erykah Badu while Rosalyn tussled with her thoughts pretending to be sleep.

43

(Episode 7)

The Sleepover

"You mean to tell me you ran right into him and you didn't even say HELLO!" shouted Zoey.

"We were just passing by. I didn't even know it was him at first," said Rosalyn unzipping her sleeping bag and crawling inside. Her parents agreed without a fuss to let her sleep over at Sharice's house.

"Yeah but when you realized it was him the cat got your tongue and you probably choked on that cheese steak you were eating," said Zoey.

"Get serious Zoey. It's not like he saved her from a burning building or something! Dang! He only held the door open for her," said Sharice just before she stuffed popcorn into her mouth.

"His DAD held the door open," Rosalyn butted in. "And it really doesn't matter. He's just a boy!"

"Yeah, a boy that happens to have a thing for you," Zoey said peering up from painting her toe nails to smile at Rosalyn.

Rosalyn's heart began to beat fast like it did after she had run into Kevin earlier that day. *There it goes again!* She thought. *You've been liked by boys before so what's the big deal?* But there was something different about this time. She had only been in town for two weeks and already a boy liked her. A boy that didn't even know her. It wasn't like the three-year crush that Jimmy Haines had on her. Everyone in Caymen Point knew Jimmy had liked her ever since they were in Mrs. Richardson's second grade class. When he finally confessed his love for her with a cheap box of jellybeans in the fifth grade, Rosalyn wasn't the least bit interested in having a boyfriend. She let him have it right in the nose and sent him home crying to his mama. But things were different. For one thing, she and Kevin were on their way to the eighth grade and the thought of him liking her certainly didn't make her want to punch him. Although, there was one thing that remained the same. She still wasn't interested in having a boyfriend. *Or was she?* Rosalyn was so deep in her thoughts that she hadn't heard Sharice talking to her.

"So, have you Rosalyn?"

"Oh. Huh? What?"

"I was asking you have you started yet?" said Sharice.

"Started what?"

"Haven't you heard anything we've been talking about for the past few minutes? We've been talking about becoming a *woman*," said Zoey. "Sharice was just asking you if you've started the big P yet?"

"Yeah, you know, your period," said Sharice.

"Oh that! Yeah, me and my best friend Monica both started last year in the sixth grade," said Rosalyn relieved that she finally knew what Sharice and Zoey were talking about.

"Well it looks like we're all on our way to becoming no-nonsense certified young ladies," said Sharice proudly. "Zoey and I started last year too."

"Hey, what do you mean no-nonsense? I hope you're not talking about that anti-boy stuff again," said Zoey.

"I'm not anti-boy. It's just that I'm too young to be getting tied down to some big-headed fool who'll only try to tell me who I can and can't hang out with and who'll want me to sit around at home all day waiting for his phone call. That's just not me. I have better things to do with my time," declared Sharice as she gave Rosalyn a high five.

"How would you know what a boyfriend wants you to do? You've never even had one," said Zoey.

"I don't have to have had one. I'm smart enough to learn from other people's mistakes, unlike yourself. Zoey, you know it's true. It happened to Felicia Barnes last year when she was going out with David Jones. After a few weeks we hardly saw heads or tail of that girl. David had her stuck to the phone like glue and didn't want her to hang out with her friends anymore. Even you get that way sometimes yourself."

47

"I do not!" shouted Zoey. "Okay, maybe once with Phillip Hardy but that's because he was so cute."

"Well I don't care how cute he is. No big-headed boy is gonna tell me what to do. I'll wait a few years for a real man, and even then he won't tell me what to do, " said Sharice as she snapped her finger in Zoey's face.

"I'm with you Sharice," Rosalyn finally said after listening to those two go at it.

Zoey rolled her eyes and shook her head in disagreement.

"Now let's change the subject," said Sharice. "This is getting boring."

"Finally," said Rosalyn ready to move on to something that didn't make her feel so uncomfortable.

"Are we trying out for the dance team this year?" asked Zoey.

Rosalyn's eyes lit up. She had been in dance classes since the age of seven, performing in everything from jazz to modern, to street style dance all over the state. Her parents had geared her into it as a way to expose her to something other than the dull suburban life they lived in Caymen Point.

"Yeah, I think we should since we chickened out last year. After seeing the girls who made the team last time, we had no reason to be afraid."

"Ain't that the truth," Zoey agreed with Sharice. "They had no rhythm at all."

"Yeah. Let's do it!" shouted Rosalyn. "I've been in dance for years. We could even make up our try out routine together."

"Well I'll say. It looks like we have a regular Janet Jackson in our corner," said Sharice.

"I'm no Janet Jackson, but I do have a few moves here and there," Rosalyn added smiling.

"Well show us what you can do Ms. Jackson," said Zoey.

"Give me a beat and I will," Rosalyn replied with confidence.

Sharice hit the power button on her stereo and a popular hip hop song came blaring from the speakers. Rosalyn stood up and went right into her favorite street dance moves. She moved to the rhythm of the song without missing a beat. At one point in her performance she even did a few moves made popular by Janet Jackson herself. Both her friends snapped their fingers to the beat and cheered her on with "Get it girl!" and "Heeeyy!". When the song ended Rosalyn struck a pose on the last beat and waited for her audience to clap like she had been taught for so many years.

"Girl where did you learn to dance like that?" asked Sharice.

"I've been in dance for six years. Those are just a *few* moves I've picked up along the way," said Rosalyn sarcastically.

After the girls calmed down from all the excitement Rosalyn had stirred up, they danced and listened to music until they fell asleep. Dance auditions for the up and coming school year were in two weeks and they were trying out.

(Episode 8)

The Talk

One evening after one of Rosalyn's mom's famous home cooked meals, Mrs. Thompson sat down on the sofa in the living room and motioned for Rosalyn to come and sit next to her. Her mother always did this when she wanted to discuss something serious or when Rosalyn was in some kind of trouble which rarely happened. She sat down slowly next to her mom and wondered what she had done to bring on the conversation that was about to happen.

"Hey mom, what's up," Rosalyn said trying to lighten the mood. Her mother looked at her and answered with a slight smile on her face.

"Nothing much. I just thought I'd sit down with my only child and have a good old fashioned mother-daughter talk."

Good, thought Rosalyn. Whatever it is, it can't be too bad because her mom was still smiling.

"I see you've been hanging out with your new friends a lot lately. It looks like you girls are getting pretty close."

"Yeah, they're cool but it's nothing like Monica and I use to be. We've decided to try out for the dance team," said Rosalyn.

"Oh Roz, that's great! I know you girls will do fine." Her mother's tone suddenly became more serious. "The real reason I wanted to talk with you is because I've noticed lately a lot of your phone conversations have a lot to do with boys which is completely normal for a young lady your age. We've already talked about what can happen when a boy and a girl get too involved so I'm not going to even go there. I do want to say though, don't ever let anyone get in your way of doing what you want to do no matter what. You can have fun and still stay focused on the big picture."

"I know all these things mama. You've already schooled me on that. Don't worry. I don't have a boyfriend. There's just some boy named Kevin who is supposed to like me, that's all. I would never let some boy or even new friends take my focus away from my grades and school."

"I know you're smart because you're my daughter but I just thought I'd remind you. I only want what's best for you sweetie."

"Ma, I already have the best. I have you," Rosalyn said smiling and giving her mother a hug. Just then the phone rang.

"I'll get it," said Rosalyn pulling away from the hug.

"Okay, but if it's one of your friends don't stay on the phone too late," her mom said looking her in the eyes with a smile.

"Okay mama." Rosalyn said running to get the phone.

"Hello."

"Hi Rosalyn. It's me Monica."

"Hi Monica!" said Rosalyn. "Girl I miss you so much!"

"I miss you too. I wanted to call you before it got too late so I could get you all caught up on the summer gossip around here. You haven't forgot about me have you?"

"No way!" Rosalyn replied. "I feel like we need to see each other."

"Me too," said Monica.

"Maybe you can come visit one weekend since summer is almost over."

"Sounds good to me," said Monica. "I'll make sure I talk to my parents about it."

"Me too," Rosalyn replied.

The girls talked for more than an hour. By the end of the conversation Rosalyn was all caught up on who liked who back in Caymen Point, who got in a fight and even who didn't pass on to the eighth grade. Rosalyn told Monica all about her new friends and how some boy she barely knew had a thing for her.

"Well it's sounds like you're adjusting to life in Sherwood pretty good," said Monica.

"I'm trying but it's not easy. Even with Zoey and Sharice as friends, sometimes I get homesick for Caymen Point."

"Maybe you'll feel better after we see each other."

"Yeah maybe you're right," said Rosalyn.

The girls said their goodbyes with a promise to get together soon. Rosalyn went to bed that night feeling good about the future. She was slowly adjusting to Sherwood and her best friend was coming to visit.

(Episode 9)

The Turning Point

It all happened so fast. No one would have seen it coming. One evening Rosalyn was in her room finally putting away some of the boxed clothes her mother had been telling her to put away for weeks when the phone rang. She decided to let her dad get it because she was too busy and her mother was gone on a catering event. The phone rang several times and still her dad didn't pick up. Rosalyn swore sometimes that man would get in front of the t.v. and end up on a whole other planet. Rosalyn sighed and ran to answer the phone.

"Hello."

"Yes, hello is this the Thompson residence?".

"Yes this is Rosalyn Thompson who is this?"

"This is the Sherwood police department. Is your father home?"

"Yeah, hold on," replied Rosalyn. "Daddy, the phone!" she yelled. "It's the police department."

"The police department?" He yelled back from downstairs.

"Yeah," said Rosalyn.

Her dad picked up the phone downstairs and Rosalyn hung up the upstairs line.

"Hello, this is Mr. Thompson."

"Mr. Thompson, this is the Sherwood police department. I'm afraid there's been an accident... It's your wife."

Her mother's death sent her into a deep depression for weeks. Everything between the phone call from the police department to the funeral and days after were a blur to Rosalyn. She remembers being awakened several times in the middle of the night by her father because she had been crying in her sleep. Rosalyn felt like she couldn't go on living. How could she? She had just lost the most important person in her life. The thought of living without her mother was unbearable. There were countless moments where her thoughts and emotions consumed her.

What will I do without my mama. It isn't fair. How could God do this to me? I thought he loved me. What about my high school graduation, college graduation, my first boyfriend, my wedding, my kids! I want to know why me of all people was chosen to go through these things without my mother. I'm a good student and I keep my room clean. I barely get into trouble. Why me? God this hurts! I love her so much! I can't handle this! My heart hurts so bad it makes me sick to my stomach! God this hurts! I want my mama!

"Rosalyn you have to eat something. It's been two weeks since you've had any real food to eat." Her grandmother, who was now staying with them forced her to eat a piece of fruit for breakfast.

"You have to eat something Rosalyn. I'm not gon' let you sit and wither away to nothing. You already skin and bones girl now eat!"

"I can't grandma. I just can't."

Sitting at the kitchen table to eat anything made her even more depressed than she already was. It made her think of how much her mother loved to cook. She put her head down on the table and began to sob.

"It's okay child," said her grandmother as she gently consoled Rosalyn's shaking shoulders. "Everything's gon' be alright but you just have to keep your head up baby. I know it's hard but your mother wouldn't want you mopin' around here like this, not eating and staying locked up in your room. She carried you for nine months and went through a lot of laboring to get you here. I don't think she'd appreciate you wasting all her hard work. You still have breath in your lungs. You still alive girl. Your mother and God gave you life and it's about time for you to start living again. No more sleeping all day. No more keeping your blinds closed. No more passing up phone calls from your friends. It's time for you to live again. That's the only way your mother would have it. Now get up and get yourself together 'cause I'm getting you out of this house today. We're goin' shopping."

Rosalyn slowly lifted her head and stopped crying. Her grandmother helped her up from the table and gave her a hug. Rosalyn held her grandma tight and suddenly started sobbing again.

"Grandma I can't do it," Rosalyn said between sobs. "I just can't go on living."

"I know it's hard honey," her grandma replied, "but you CAN do it. You just don't know it yet. God never gives you more than you can handle."

They held each other for a few moments and then her grandma slowly pulled back from the hug. She gently wiped Roslayn's tears, and with tears in her own eyes she softly said, "You can do this baby. I'll be with you every step of the way. Now go get dressed."

Before they did any serious shopping, her grandmother insisted they get what she called *the royal treatment* at the shopping mall salon. She went up to the counter and put in her request.

"Hey Antoine, how you doin'?"

"Well look who's here. My most favorite glamour girl in the whole world, Mrs. Thompson. I'm doin' fabulous. Where've you been beautiful?"

"Oh I've been around. Just hangin' out with my granddaughter. Rosalyn this is Antoine. Antoine meet my beautiful granddaughter Rosalyn."

"Well hello there gorgeous."

"Hi," Rosalyn replied in a low voice.

"So, what can I do for you two young ladies today?"

"We'd like to have the works today if it's not too much trouble," said Mrs. Thompson.

"Too much trouble? Well honey of course not. It's not every day I get to make two gorgeous young ladies even more gorgeous," said Antoine as he cheerfully led them to the back to get started.

Rosalyn thought he was just a little too happy for it to be only ten o' clock in the morning. He must really love his job.

He started by giving them both a pedicure. Rosalyn didn't see why people made such a big deal out of getting their feet done. She felt there was nothing glamorous or exciting about having someone dig in between your toes and scrub all the dead skin from the bottom of your feet. Next he gave them facials while some red-haired, gum-popping lady with a huge gap in between her two front teeth did their manicures.

"This sure does feel good," said Rosalyn's grandma. "Don't you think so Rosalyn?"

"It's okay," replied Rosalyn.

"Okay? If it's just okay then we're not doing our jobs little Ms. Rosalyn," Antoine responded.

"Oh don't mind her Antoine. Lately Rosalyn's been feeling a little down. Hopefully today we can get her to feel as beautiful on the inside as she is on the outside."

"Well you've come the right place," said Antoine.

He finished up their facials then looked at Rosalyn from the corner of his eye and gave a huge smile.

"I know just what to do to make a gorgeous young lady like you feel gorgeous."

He turned Rosalyn around in the swivel chair away from the mirror to face him. With a big makeup brush he began to lightly blend a bronze blusher over her cheeks and forehead. He then gently applied a touch of mascara to each set of her eyelashes and topped off her new face with a thin layer of mango peach flavored lip gloss. Lastly, he swept her hanging braids up into a neat bun with a rhinestone butterfly hair clip. When Antoine finished, he slowly turned Rosalyn back around toward the mirror to look at herself.

Rosalyn looked in the mirror at herself and saw a different person. It was the prettiest she had ever seen herself look and she liked it. What seemed like endless days of mourning her mother's death, dodging her friends and staying locked up in her room didn't matter at this moment. What mattered to her right now at this very moment was that she felt alive again. Like she could actually go on living.

"You look beautiful," her grandmother said with tears in her eyes.

"I do look okay don't I," Rosalyn said looking in the mirror at herself smiling.

"Honey you look better than okay. You look fabulous!" shouted Antoine.

Rosalyn and Mrs. Thompson graciously thanked Antoine for his services after he made them promise to come and see him at least once a month. Then they finally got down to the business of some serious shopping.

When they finished, Rosalyn had three new outfits with shoes to match, a new cd, two pairs of earrings and a gold charm necklace. They decided to finish off their day of pampering and shopping with eating at the mall buffet. As they finished their meal and began to make their way out of the restaurant and back out into the mall, Rosalyn thought she heard someone calling her name. She turned and looked around. It was Zoey and Sharice.

"Rosalyn, wait up!" shouted Sharice.

As the two girls quickly approached her, Zoey was limping. They ran up to her and hugged her simultaneously.

"Oh my god Rosalyn we've missed you so much!" said Sharice. "We heard about your mom and have been trying to call you for days."

"I know you have and I'm sorry I didn't call back," said Rosalyn. "It's been rough for me lately but I think I'll be okay."

"So does that mean we can hang again?" said Zoey.

"Yes, that's exactly what that means," Rosalyn's grandma replied eagerly. She had been happily watching and listening to the girls reunite with one another.

"Can we start by getting a ride home *please* Mrs. Thompson? My feet are killing me!" cried Zoey.

"Nobody told you to try and be cute and wear those heels to the mall."

"Oh shut up already Sharice."

"You two are still the same," laughed Rosalyn.

They sang loudly to the radio all the way home but Rosalyn's grandma didn't mind a bit. She was just glad to see her granddaughter laugh again.

(Episode 10)

Tryouts

"So what's up? Are we still trying out for the dance team or not," asked Sharice.

"I think we should," answered Zoey. "Like I said before, those poor girls from last year didn't have a lick of rhythm. I know we're better than them and besides, it'll be good for my social life to be known as one of the prime dancers on campus."

"I'm not looking to be known as some wanna be video dancer," snapped Sharice. "I just wanna have some fun that's all."

"Rosalyn you're awfully quiet over there. What do you think we should do?"

"Well Zoey, since we only have a few days before tryouts I don't know if we can put something together in time. Even with my experience, it takes time to make up a routine and then perfect it enough to tryout with it."

"Girl are you doubting our skills! We can do this. We've got what it takes," encouraged Sharice.

Rosalyn looked at both of them thoughtfully. "Maybe you're right. Let's do it!", she said.

"Yeah, let's do this girls!" agreed Zoey.

Rosalyn, Zoey and Sharice arrived at their school gym on the morning of tryouts both nervous and eager to get things under way. It was hot and crowded in the gym. It was filled with onlooking parents, girls and even a few boys that were trying out for the dance team. There were some in groups practicing their routines and some by themselves in corners or with on-looking parents shouting words of encouragement.

"Okay girls, we got this!" said Rosalyn to the other two.

"Umm… I don't know Roz. This crowd looks pretty good compared to last year's," Sharice said as she glanced around the gym.

"Yeah," Zoey agreed with Sharice.

"Oh uhnn uhnn! I know you two aren't doubting our skills!" replied Rosalyn surprised.

Just then the "goonie bunch" that had given Rosalyn a hard time at the skating rink walked by and rolled their eyes at the three of them.

"What's their problem?" snapped Sharice. "Ooooh, we are gonna really have to turn it up now girls. There is no way I'm gonna let those little groupies intimidate me."

"Exactly!" said Rosalyn. "Let's show these girls we didn't come to play. Zoey, you in?" Rosalyn's competitive dance spirit was beginning to show.

"I guess so, but I hope you two know what you're doing. I don't need something like not making the dance team to be a part of my eighth grade reputation."

"Girl would you stop worrying about your rep for a minute and think about your pride for once," said Rosalyn. "Like I said before, let's show these girls we didn't come to play!"

"...*and boys*," Sharice butted in.

Before tryouts began, one of the organizers made all the dancers pull numbers to see what order they would go in. It turns out Sharice would be the first of the three to tryout then Rosalyn and lastly Zoey. When it was Zoey's turn Rosalyn and Sharice had to encourage her to go through with it.

"You guise, I don't think I can do this," Zoey said rubbing her hands together nervously.

"Yes you can Zoey," said Rosalyn.

"It actually wasn't that bad," said Sharice. "Just look at the judge in the middle. That's the one that kept smiling at me."

"At me too," said Rosalyn. "I'm telling you, you got this Zoey. Trust me. I know. Now go because they've already called your number twice."

"Alright," said Zoey as she slowly started to make her way to the tryout room. Just before she went in, she looked back at Rosalyn and Sharice. They both smiled and gave her the thumbs up sign. Five minutes later she came running out huffing and puffing.

"Oh my God! That was one of the hardest things I've ever done in my life but I think I nailed It!"

"See, I told you!" the other two girls shouted in unison.

It turns out tryouts went well for all three girls. At the end, when names were called for those who made the team, Rosalyn, Sharice and Zoey were thrilled that they all had made it. The rest of the team consisted of two girls from the "goonie bunch" named Simone and Shawntelle, one incoming sixth grader named Melanie, two seventh graders named Princess and Talia and an eighth grade boy named Delano.

After the names were called, Rosalyn continued to sit staring, thinking about her mother while others were leaving. She wished her mother was there so she could share the good news with her. Mrs. Thompson had been so excited when Rosalyn told her that she and the girls were trying out for the dance team. Rosalyn knows she would have been overjoyed about them making it. Tears began to well up in her eyes.

"Roz, are you okay?" said Sharice. "Girl we made the team. That's good news."

"I know," she responded. "I was just thinking about how my mama would have loved to see us dance on the team. She was so happy when I told her about us trying out."

"Well then," said Zoey while putting her arm around Rosalyn's shoulder. "I guess we'll just have to dedicate this season to your mom."

Rosalyn slowly looked at Zoey and replied, "I like that. Yes. To my mama."

"Yes, to Rosalyn's mama," added Sharice softly.

The girls stood up and walked out the gym arm in arm smiling. School would be starting soon and they were on the dance team.

www.ingramcontent.com/pod-product-compliance
Lightning Source LLC
Chambersburg PA
CBHW022051170626
46808CB00003B/1440